SAGAR J. THUMMAR

Room 115: Secrets of the Haunted Orphanage

Contents

Prologue

The night was thick with fog, a heavy blanket that swallowed the path leading up to the old orphanage. Its towering, decaying walls loomed against the dark sky, a forgotten relic of the past. The air was damp, carrying with it an eerie stillness, as if the world had paused just to listen to the whispers that echoed from within the walls of the orphanage.

Once a thriving home for children, the orphanage had been abandoned for decades. No one had dared to live there since the terrible events that took place within its cold, crumbling halls. But tonight, the orphanage wasn't silent. It waited.

Room 115.

That was the room everyone in town avoided. It had always been locked, its door sealed shut for as long as anyone could remember. Those who dared to venture near the room spoke of strange noises—whispers, cries, and sometimes, the unmistakable sound of children laughing. But these were no ordinary sounds. They were the sounds of something that had never truly left.

Kiara Sharma's heart pounded as she stared at the building. Her curiosity had led her here, driven by the strange letter she had found, one that spoke of the orphanage's dark past and the hidden secrets it held. The letter had been written years ago by a child who had died in the orphanage, someone who had suffered the horrors of an experiment gone horribly wrong.

Kiara had gathered her friends—Aarav, Kabir, Vivaan, and Meher—to help her uncover the truth. But they were unaware of the deep and terrifying history they were about to uncover.

As they crossed the broken gates, the wind seemed to grow colder, sharper, like it had a warning to give. The orphanage's once grand entrance now stood as a shadow of its former self—torn banners fluttering in the wind, windows shattered like broken memories.

Kiara's steps were slow but determined. She was no stranger to fear, but there was something about this place, something that made her skin crawl and her breath catch in her throat. The others followed, exchanging uneasy glances, their nerves visible in the way they shifted their weight from foot to foot.

They reached the main door, its once polished wood now chipped and worn, as if time itself had tried to forget the horrors inside. Kiara pushed it open, the rusty hinges creaking like the groan of something ancient awakening from a long slumber.

The smell hit them first—dust, mildew, and something else… something that made their stomachs churn. But it was more than just the physical decay. There was a presence here, something intangible, lurking in the dark corners of the orphanage.

The hallway stretched out before them, dimly lit by the faintest glow of light that slipped through the cracks in the boarded-up windows. The walls were covered in peeling paint, and the floor beneath their feet creaked ominously as if protesting their intrusion.

"Kiara, are you sure about this?" Aarav asked, his voice barely above a whisper. He was the first to speak, though the tension in the air made his words feel like a shout.

Kiara nodded, her eyes never leaving the long, dark hallway.

"We need to find the truth. This place… it's hiding something. Something important."

As they made their way deeper into the orphanage, the silence grew heavier, more oppressive. The walls seemed to close in around them, the shadows stretching and shifting as if they had a life of their own.

They reached the stairs, their footsteps echoing in the stillness. The higher they climbed, the colder the air became, until it felt like they were walking through a winter night.

At the top of the stairs, they stopped in front of a door. There, above the doorframe, was the number "115" etched into the wood, its faded lines barely visible in the dim light. Kiara's heart raced as she reached for the doorknob, her fingers trembling.

But before she could touch it, a faint sound echoed from within the room—a child's laugh. It was high-pitched, eerie, and distant, like it came from a place far beyond time.

The laughter stopped abruptly, replaced by the soft rustling of fabric. A voice—quiet, almost like a whisper on the wind— drifted through the door.

"You shouldn't have come."

The words were chilling, as if they were spoken from a place where the line between the living and the dead no longer existed.

Kiara's breath caught in her throat. "We have to go in," she said, more to herself than to anyone else.

Aarav stepped forward, hesitating for a moment before grabbing the handle and turning it. The door creaked open, revealing a room that was frozen in time. Dusty old furniture, abandoned toys scattered across the floor, and in the center of the room, a faded photograph hanging crookedly on the wall.

The photograph showed a group of children, their faces

smiling, but their eyes—those eyes—were filled with a sadness that reached out from the past.

Kiara stepped further into the room, her eyes drawn to the picture. "This is it," she whispered. "This is where it all started."

As she looked around, she could feel the presence of something—someone—watching her, waiting for her to uncover the truth. The room seemed to close in on her, the air thick with memories, sorrow, and regret.

She didn't know it yet, but what they were about to uncover would shake them to their core. The orphanage's dark past, the horrors hidden within the walls, and the terrifying truth about Room 115 were waiting for them. And once they learned it, there would be no turning back.

Room 115 was waiting.

1

The Letter That Started It All

It was a cloudy Friday afternoon in Mumbai, and the sky looked as if it was ready to cry. The last bell of St. Mary's college echoed through the corridors like a slow drum, and excited students rushed out with noisy chatter and swinging backpacks.

But one person stayed behind.

Kiara Sharma sat alone at the corner table of the school library. Around her, tall wooden shelves stood like silent giants, filled with forgotten books. The air smelled of old paper and dust. A faint flickering from the tube light above her added an eerie rhythm to the silence.

Kiara was not your regular college student. She was bold, smart, and different. While others gossiped about weekend plans, Kiara was flipping through a thick book titled *"India's Forgotten Homes"*. Her fingers moved slowly, her eyes sharp, like a detective searching for hidden clues.

Suddenly, a faint *thud* broke the silence.

One of the pages had loosened, and something fell out. Kiara picked it up.

It was an **old, yellowed envelope** with no stamp, no proper name—just five words in faded ink:

"To the one who dares to know the truth."

Her heartbeat quickened.

She looked around. The librarian was nowhere to be seen. Slowly, carefully, she opened the envelope. Inside was a fragile letter, folded neatly but stained at the corners—like someone had held it with trembling fingers.

She unfolded it, and her eyes scanned the writing. It was messy, almost childlike:

**"They said they would make us stronger.

They said it was just a medicine.

But we were not sick.

Why did they choose us?

I miss Raghav.

He cried all night, but no one came.

Then he stopped crying.

He never woke up.

Room 115 is cursed.

Don't let them forget what they did.

Please… tell the world.

— Myra"**

Kiara stared at the letter. A chill crawled down her spine.

She touched the paper again—there were faint **water stains**… or were they **teardrops**?

She quickly took photos on her phone and placed the letter back into the book as it was. Something told her… this wasn't just some prank. It felt *real*—as if the letter itself still carried the pain of the child who wrote it.

That evening, back in her room, Kiara couldn't sleep.

The words haunted her. *"They said it was medicine... Room 115 is cursed."*

She turned on her laptop and began researching. Her room was dark except for the blue glow of the screen. She typed quickly:

"Room 115 orphanage Mumbai"

"Myra orphanage experiment"

"Raghav child death Mumbai orphanage"

"Illegal medical experiments India"

Most links led to dead ends or old news. But one article caught her attention.

It was a decade-old blog post by an anonymous source:

*"In 2009, a private foundation known as **Proton Foundation** shut down its children's orphanage outside Mumbai after multiple 'suspicious' deaths. No official cause was ever revealed. Locals believe Room 115 was sealed forever after a major accident involving fire and toxic gas."*

Kiara's eyes widened. *Proton Foundation. Room 115. Suspicious deaths.*

It was not just a story anymore—it was a *truth buried in silence.*

She sent urgent texts to her close friends:

"Meet at Café Kumbh, 8PM sharp. Found something BIG. Don't ignore."

Later that evening – Café Kumbh

The café was small and quiet, with dim yellow lights and wooden walls covered in art. Outside, the rain had started again, tapping on the glass windows like a soft warning.

One by one, Kiara's friends arrived.

Aarav Mehra came first, confident and calm, always ready for an adventure. He gave Kiara a side hug.

Kabir Khan, the group's sarcastic realist, walked in complaining, "I hope this isn't another ghost theory of yours."

Vivaan Malhotra, the quiet science enthusiast, brought his tablet and sat without saying much, already curious.

Meher Roy, spiritual and soft-spoken, walked in silently, holding a small diary with a moon drawn on the cover.

Kiara wasted no time.

She placed the printed copy of the letter on the table.

"This was hidden in a book in our school library. It's not just a letter—it's a cry for help."

They all leaned in and read the note.

Silence followed.

"I have a bad feeling already," Meher whispered.

Vivaan looked thoughtful. "Did you say... they gave 'medicine'? That sounds like some kind of biological trial."

Kiara nodded. "Yes. And the Proton Foundation might have been running experiments on orphan kids. That orphanage—where this Myra and Raghav stayed—it was shut down quietly, no real records, no clear reason. But it's there. Still standing. And Room 115 is real."

Kabir shook his head. "I don't know. You really think someone experimented on kids here? That's dark, even for India."

Aarav stared at the letter. "It doesn't matter what we think. If this is even partly true... someone needs to know."

Vivaan opened his tablet. "If they were testing some kind of gene-altering substance—maybe a serum to increase immunity or intelligence—it could have side effects. Children are more sensitive to those things. One wrong step, and..."

He didn't finish the sentence.

Meher touched the letter gently. "This pain... it's still here. I feel it."

Kiara looked at them, serious and sharp. "I'm going to the orphanage tomorrow. It's a few hours away, abandoned. But I'll go. With or without you."

Aarav immediately responded. "We're coming with you."

Kabir rolled his eyes. "Fine. But if I get cursed, I'm blaming all of you."

Vivaan gave a quiet nod. "I need to see this. From a scientific point of view."

Meher, her voice barely a whisper, said, "Something is waiting for us there. I saw it last night… in my dream."

Kiara looked around the table. Her heart was racing—not with fear, but determination.

They didn't know what waited in that broken orphanage.

But one thing was sure.

They had just opened the door to a past that refused to stay buried.

And in the shadows of **Room 115**, someone… or something… was still watching.

End of Chapter 1

2

Journey to the Orphanage

The morning sky was grey, like someone had pulled a blanket of smoke over the city. Clouds hung low, heavy with secrets. A light drizzle coated the streets as five determined shadows moved quietly through the mist—Kiara, Aarav, Kabir, Vivaan, and Meher.

They had packed light: flashlights, first-aid kit, snacks, a handheld video camera, an old map, and a notebook. Vivaan also brought a portable chemical trace detector—small, square, with blinking green lights. "If something was used during the experiment," he said, "it might still leave a residue."

The orphanage stood far from the city, lost in silence, hidden by wild forests. It had been shut for over a decade. No official reports, no public record. Just whispers.

The Train Ride and The Unease
They boarded the train at CST station. Their destination: **Vasarpada**, a forgotten village on the city's edge. The coach was nearly empty. As the train moved, the tension inside the group grew louder than the engine.

Kiara sat near the window, fingers tracing droplets on the fogged glass. She kept replaying the lines from the letter in her mind—Myra's words, raw and scared.

Beside her, Meher whispered, "She called out to me again last night."

Kiara turned, concerned. "Myra?"

"She was crying. Saying… they put something in her. Something alive. Her skin was burning from inside."

Kiara swallowed. Even Kabir looked uncomfortable hearing that.

Aarav tried to lighten the mood. "Don't tell me ghosts are haunting dreams now."

"They are," Meher said softly, her eyes distant.

Vivaan interrupted. "I did some digging. Proton Foundation had a lab connected to this orphanage. They were researching something called *neural gene regulators*. They used viral vectors—like modified viruses—to carry synthetic genes into the children's bodies."

"Why would they do that?" Aarav asked.

"To enhance cognition," Vivaan explained, "maybe create children with sharper memory, faster thinking. But if the genes mutated or were rejected by the body, the result could be… fatal."

"Playing God," Kabir said grimly.

The Forest and the Sound

They reached Vasarpada station. The platform was cracked and overgrown. Nature had claimed it back.

The group started walking through the forest trail. Trees stood tall like silent witnesses. A light mist hugged the ground. As they walked deeper, **a strange sound filled the air**—a high-pitched humming.

"What is that?" Vivaan asked, turning.

"I hear it too," Meher whispered. "It's not wind."

"It's like… crying," she added after a pause. "Low and steady. She's calling."

Kiara stopped. "Let's keep moving."

The Arrival

After nearly an hour, they reached a rusted iron gate. Behind it loomed a tall, broken building with shattered windows, a half-collapsed roof, and faded paint.

A rusted board read:

"BAL KALYAN KENDRA – Supported by Proton Foundation"

The last line was barely visible.

They climbed through a broken section of the wall and stepped onto the dead campus. The air was heavy. It smelled of mold, rust, and something metallic—like old blood.

Inside the Orphanage

The hallway was long and narrow. Light from their flashlights flickered on cracked walls and dusty tiles. A broken tricycle lay in one corner. Children's artwork still hung crooked on the walls—stick figures, flowers, stars, and one drawing of a black sun.

Vivaan switched on his detector.

BEEP.

The light on the screen turned amber.

"What is it?" Kiara asked.

"Chemical trace," Vivaan said, puzzled. "Still active. Could be residue from a compound—maybe viral. It shouldn't exist after this many years unless it was… absorbed into the walls."

Everyone fell silent.

They turned down the hallway labeled "Block A." The room numbers passed slowly: 109… 110… 114… and then—**115.**

Room 115

The door was swollen and dark, wood splintered like claws had scratched it. As Kiara touched the knob, a cold sensation ran up her arm.

Aarav pushed the door open.

The room was silent. Dead.

There was one bed. One broken chair. On the far wall, smeared with a black, crusted substance, was a **child's drawing**.

It showed five children standing under a tree. One child was violently **crossed out in red**—head scratched out, body torn. Below it were the words:

"Don't forget me."

Suddenly, Meher gasped.

Her body stiffened. Eyes rolled back. Her voice turned… childlike.

"They hurt me. I begged them. I screamed. They didn't stop. I want to go home. I want to go hoooome—"

Aarav rushed forward. "Meher!"

Kiara held her. "Snap out of it!"

Meher blinked. Then collapsed into their arms, sweating. "She's here," she whispered. "Watching us."

Kabir stumbled over something on the ground—a dusty old **tape recorder**.

He picked it up, wiped it, and pressed play.

It whirred. Static.

Then a voice.

Low. Broken. Barely audible:

"Room... one... fifteen..."

The tape stopped.

No one moved.

The Presence

A sudden gust of wind slammed the door shut behind them.

The flashlight flickered.

On the wall, written faintly in chalk now glowing in their torchlight:

"They said it was medicine... but it burned like fire."

Kiara felt her chest tighten. Her throat dry.

She stared into the shadows of Room 115... and there, in the far corner, she thought she saw **a girl**.

Barefoot. Pale. Hair over her face.

Just standing there.

End of Chapter 2

3

The First Signs

The air inside the orphanage was different now. Thicker. Heavier. As if time had slowed down and the walls were breathing.

The five students—Kiara, Aarav, Kabir, Vivaan, and Meher— had split up to explore different parts of the building, their torches flickering in the dark like fireflies caught in a web.

Kiara stood near a cracked hallway mirror, staring at her reflection. Behind her, the corridor stretched on forever—or so it felt. She heard faint whispers, too soft to make out, like a child talking to themselves. When she turned around, there was nothing but silence.

Vivaan was in the biology lab, brushing dust off a long-abandoned shelf. His modified biosensor suddenly blinked red.

"Unstable compound detected," the screen read.

He narrowed his eyes. *That's not normal.*

Myra's Drawing on the Wall
Meher, who had been following a strange cold spot, stepped

into an old dormitory. The wallpaper was peeling, and broken beds lined the walls. Something drew her to the far end.

There, hidden behind a torn curtain, was a **child's drawing scratched into the wall** with what looked like fingernails.

It showed a girl—small, with braids—sitting in a room numbered **115.** Red marks surrounded her. Over her head was a hand—black, with claws.

Meher's breath hitched. "It's Myra…"

The chalk mark began to bleed. Right in front of her.

Vivaan's Device Reacts Again

Vivaan had barely moved from the lab when his device buzzed again. It now read:

"Neurotoxin residue – expired strain."

"What the hell?" he muttered.

He leaned closer to a rusted cabinet. Inside were broken vials. One still had liquid in it, marked **PF-7X.** He tried to photograph it, but the moment he pressed the button, the camera shut off.

Suddenly, the temperature dropped. Behind him, a mirror cracked—no impact, no sound—just shattered slowly as if under pressure.

Vivaan turned to the mirror. In the web of cracks, for a second, he saw a **figure with glowing white eyes and no mouth** standing behind him.

He spun around. No one.

Meher's Possession-like Episode

Meher's scream echoed down the corridor. The others rushed to find her lying on the floor, eyes rolled back, whispering in a hoarse voice:

"He is watching… He never left… Room Zero… Room Zero…

It's not on the map…"

Her voice wasn't hers.

Kiara knelt beside her. "Meher! Wake up!"

Aarav splashed water on her. Meher gasped back to life, shaking.

"I-I didn't feel like myself," she said, trembling. "Something tried to enter me. It was angry. Not like Myra or the others… This one hates us."

Kabir frowned. "Wait. Who else is here?"

They all looked at each other in silence.

The Broken Tape Recorder

They decided to check the warden's old office next. The door was slightly ajar, creaking open with a push. On the desk was a broken tape recorder covered in dust.

Kiara pressed the button. Static.

Then suddenly—a whisper:

"Don't dig… Don't uncover… It lives here."

A loud screech came from the tape, and the recorder sparked and died.

Kabir stepped back. "Okay, I'm done pretending this place is just haunted. Something doesn't want us here."

The Forest Sound

As night fell, they heard it—the sound of **something dragging across the forest floor** outside. Not an animal. Too heavy. Too human.

Aarav peered through a cracked window. He saw movement— just beyond the trees. A figure. Not Myra. Not a child. Taller. Broken in posture. Watching the house.

It disappeared into the shadows.

"What was that?" Kiara whispered.

"I don't know," he replied. "But it's not a victim. It's something else…"

Back Inside – Evidence Vanishes

When they returned to the biology lab, the vial Vivaan found was gone. The drawer? Blown open, its contents shredded.

Kabir checked his camera footage. Corrupted. But for one brief second—just before the distortion—a single frame flashed:

A silhouette. Glowing eyes. Claw-like hand. Standing in the hallway.

As they gathered in the main hall again, Meher whispered, "Something here is **guarding** the truth. It doesn't want us to know."

Kiara clutched Myra's letter tighter.

"No matter what's here… we're not leaving. Not until we know everything."

End of Chapter 3

4

The Hidden Room

The orphanage had secrets. But this one... it didn't want to be found.

The morning was dull and gray. No birds chirped outside, and the usual forest breeze had turned still, like nature itself was holding its breath. The group gathered at the main staircase, still shaken from the night's terrifying experiences.

Kiara laid out the map of the orphanage they had found tucked inside an old physics textbook from the library. Everyone leaned in.

"There's a blank section here," she said, tapping a faded area between the east and west wings. "It doesn't match the building's structure. There must be a room behind that wall."

"Room Zero," Meher whispered. "That's what I said when I was... taken over."

Kabir nodded, unusually quiet. "It's worth checking. Whatever's there, they didn't want anyone to find it."

Finding the Hidden Entrance

The group followed the map's directions toward the

basement—an area they hadn't dared to enter yet. The narrow stairs were crumbling, and every step echoed like a scream down the cold corridor.

Vivaan swept his biosensor along the damp walls. Nothing. Nothing… and then—**a beep**.

"Pressure inconsistency behind this wall," he said, pointing to a moldy surface. "There's space behind here."

Aarav knocked. *Hollow.*

Kabir pushed a wooden cabinet aside, revealing a barely visible outline of a **sealed door**, plastered over with bricks and cement.

"Someone really didn't want this door to open," Kiara muttered.

They began pulling away the bricks with metal rods and their bare hands. As they worked, the air grew heavier.

Suddenly—**Meher jerked back**, holding her head. "I hear screams… so many… children crying… it's coming from inside."

Aarav finally cracked open the lock. Dust burst into the air.

They had found it—**Room Zero.**

Inside Room Zero

The door creaked open to reveal **a long corridor**, narrower than expected. On each side, rusted doors lined the walls like an old hospital wing.

Each door had a number.

115

115

115

Every room was labeled **Room 115**.

"Why the same number?" Aarav whispered.

Vivaan checked his device. "The radiation level is abnormally high here. This was used for biological tests. The levels are still detectable after all these years."

They opened the first door slowly.

Inside was a tiny room. A rusted bed. Blood-stained white walls. A steel tray with empty vials. And in the corner, a small **stuffed bunny**, half burnt.

Meher stepped inside and gasped.

"This was Myra's. She mentioned this toy in her letter."

Kiara picked up an old report lying near the bed—half-torn, faded.

"Subject 7: Myra Verma. Initial results show increased cognitive sensitivity. However, emotional instability and hallucinations observed after second dose of PF-7X."

Vivaan read it again. "They experimented with drug trials… PF-7X. This was the prototype formula. Designed for brain enhancement but… it caused severe neurological damage."

Kabir looked disturbed. "They used her like a lab rat."

The Files and the Warning

In the fourth Room 115, they found an old **filing cabinet** rusted shut. Aarav forced it open. Inside were folders labeled:

- **Project Guardian - Phase 1**
- **Neural Trigger Testing**
- **Emergency Shutdown Protocol**

And one file marked in red:

"WARNING: DO NOT RELEASE SUBJECT 12."

Vivaan opened it. The pages were stuck with dried blood.

It mentioned a test subject who showed extreme resistance to control, displayed violent behaviour, and disrupted equipment.

"Subject 12 does not respond to sedation. Appears to communicate with unknown energy fields. Facility evacuation suggested. Status: CONTAINED in Sub-Room B."

"Could this be the **unknown ghost**?" Kiara whispered.

"We need to find Sub-Room B," Aarav said, his jaw tight.

The Unmarked Door

At the end of the corridor, a rusted iron door had no handle. Only a symbol carved deep into it—a circle with a slash through it. Forbidden.

The moment they approached it, **Vivaan's device exploded with static.**

The lights flickered. Meher collapsed again, her eyes rolling back.

"He waits… he guards… truth must die with him… you cannot free what was never born…"

A gust of freezing wind howled through the corridor. The door rattled violently, as if something inside was slamming against it.

They pulled Meher away.

"Whatever is inside," Kabir said, "it's not Myra. It's something else."

Kiara closed the file tightly.

"And it's hiding the truth from the world."

An Emotional Truth

They returned to the main hall, shaken.

Kiara sat silently, holding the bunny, staring into the distance. "Myra was a bright child… They promised her safety, food, a future… and turned her into a monster."

Meher whispered, "She never became a monster… They did."

Tears welled up in Kiara's eyes.

"I won't let her death be in vain. We'll find out everything. Even if it kills us."

End of Chapter 4

5

The Scientist's Secret

The hidden room behind the cracked wall had left them shaken. Blood-written words, strange ritual markings, and the sudden appearance of a terrifying ghost that wasn't Myra—it was all too much. But what disturbed them most was the message carved in dried blood:

"You were warned. Truth dies here."

They had to find out what had really happened in the orphanage, beyond what the walls whispered. The only person who could tell them more was **Dr. Arjun Rathod**, the former scientist at **Proton Foundation**—a man whose name was buried in dusty records and half-burnt files.

A Mysterious Journey Begins

Early the next morning, Kiara, Aarav, Kabir, Vivaan, and Meher sat in the common area of their dormitory. A cloudy sky hung above them, thunder rumbling like a distant warning.

Kiara was restless, pacing the floor. "He's our only lead," she said, holding a printout of Dr. Rathod's last known address.

Kabir frowned. "What if he doesn't want to talk?"

Vivaan adjusted his specs. "Then we make him talk. He was part of something evil. He owes the truth to the world."

Meher, sitting quietly until now, suddenly whispered, "I… saw something last night."

Everyone turned to her.

"Myra was crying. She was standing outside my window. And then… she pointed in the direction of the city. I think… she wants us to meet Dr. Rathod."

That was enough. Without another word, the group left the orphanage grounds, sneaking past the watchtower where **Mr. Tiwari**, the warden, dozed with a half-empty cup of chai.

Dr. Rathod's House

They reached the address by late afternoon. The house was located in a nearly-abandoned colony on the edge of town, surrounded by dried trees and silence. The gate creaked as they pushed it open. Moss had swallowed the walls. Windows were covered in grime. A broken nameplate barely read: **Dr. A. Rathod**.

They knocked.

No response.

Kiara tried the door. It opened.

Inside, the smell was strange—a mix of antiseptic, burnt metal, and something rotting. Old x-rays, brain scans, and childlike scribbles were scattered everywhere. A broken microscope lay on the floor beside a stack of Proton Foundation files.

Vivaan picked up a photo frame from the ground. The glass was shattered. It showed a much younger Rathod with a little girl—smiling.

"This must be his daughter," Vivaan said. "Maybe that's why he quit…"

Suddenly, footsteps. The floor creaked.

Dr. Arjun Rathod stood in the hallway, eyes sunken, beard long and unkempt, like a man who hadn't slept in years.

"You shouldn't have come," he said in a broken voice.

"But we had to," Kiara replied. "Myra… the orphanage… the experiments. Please. We need to know everything."

Dr. Rathod's Breakdown

He stared at them in silence before motioning them to sit. He moved slowly, like his body carried the weight of memories he never wanted to relive.

He sat in front of them, pulled up his sleeve, and revealed deep scars on his arm—ugly, uneven, and angry.

"This… was my punishment," he said. "For watching them die and doing nothing."

Meher looked away, her hands trembling.

He opened a rusted drawer and took out an old tape recorder. With a shaking hand, he pressed play.

[TAPE RECORDING BEGINS]

"Doctor… it hurts. I can hear them even when I close my eyes. Please, make it stop…"

[SOBS]

"There's someone standing beside my bed every night. He has no face."

The tape clicked off. The silence afterward was louder than the sound.

"That was Myra… the night before she died," he said, tears gathering in his eyes.

Scientific Clarity with Simplicity

Vivaan cleared his throat. "We found documents. PF-7X.

What was it?"

Dr. Rathod leaned back, defeated. "It was supposed to be a miracle. A compound that enhanced brain function, helped with trauma, repaired memory loss. But the human brain is not a lab."

He looked at them, then pointed at a whiteboard filled with complex diagrams.

"PF-7X didn't just stimulate neurons. It *opened* them—too much. Especially in children. Their minds… started picking up things. Frequencies. Sounds. Voices. Memories that weren't theirs."

Vivaan tried to explain in simple words for the group.

"Imagine the mind like a radio. The chemical turned it into a super antenna. It started receiving signals from places… we're not supposed to hear."

"They became windows," Rathod whispered. "And something looked back."

Hint of the Unknown Ghost

Suddenly, a loud **metal dragging sound** echoed from the hallway.

Everyone froze.

Kabir stood up. "What the hell was that?"

Dr. Rathod turned pale. "It followed you."

"What do you mean?" Kiara asked.

"There was something… something that came *after* Myra died. Not part of the experiments. Not a child. Not human. It arrived when the children started dying. It lives to guard the truth. It lives to punish those who seek it."

The noise came again. A raspy breath behind a storage room door.

"Don't open that door," Rathod warned. "It doesn't like visitors. Especially ones trying to dig up the past."

Aarav stepped back as the door handle moved slightly—just once—like something inside was waiting… watching.

Meher grabbed Kiara's hand. "Let's go."

Rathod gave them one last piece of paper—an old map of the orphanage. It had a red circle on it.

"Room 115," he said. "That's where it all ends."

End of Chapter 5

6

Deeper into Darkness

The map trembled slightly in Aarav's hand as they stood outside Dr. Rathod's gate. The sky had darkened, though it was still afternoon. Thick clouds gathered like watchers above them. The silence wasn't peaceful—it was heavy. Kiara kept glancing over her shoulder. Even though they had left the house far behind, the feeling of being followed didn't leave them.

In her mind, Dr. Rathod's final words echoed again and again: "Room 115... That's where it all ends."

A Tense Return

Back at the orphanage, the air was different. Colder. Still.

As they passed through the rusting iron gates, **Vivaan's biological scanner**, a small device he had built using basic neuro-frequency detection sensors, started beeping softly. The device wasn't reacting before—not even near the ghostly sites they had explored. But now, near the orphanage, its red light blinked continuously.

Kabir raised an eyebrow. "Vivaan, that thing has never made this sound before."

"It's picking up something strange," Vivaan said quietly, adjusting its settings. "Some kind of neurological disturbance… like brainwaves, but scattered."

"Are you saying it's reading ghosts?" Aarav asked, half-serious, half-nervous.

"No. I'm saying it's reading something that shouldn't be alive."

Midnight Meeting in the Study Room

That night, Kiara called the group into the old study room. She spread the orphanage map across the dusty table. The red circle drawn by Dr. Rathod clearly marked a small room in the east wing: **Room 115**. Oddly, that room wasn't in the current blueprint of the orphanage.

Meher looked uneasy. "I've been near that wing… it's always locked. Even Mr. Tiwari avoids it."

"That's exactly where we need to go," Kiara said. "Tomorrow night. When everyone's asleep."

Kabir frowned. "So what's the plan? Break into the forbidden part of a haunted orphanage where a secret experiment killed kids and a faceless ghost protects the truth?"

Kiara smiled slightly. "Exactly."

The Descent into Room 115

At 2 a.m., the group gathered with flashlights, a toolkit, Vivaan's scanner, and a single walkie-talkie tuned to a closed channel. The orphanage was silent. Even the trees outside stood still, as if holding their breath.

The hallway to the east wing had been sealed with wooden boards, nailed in hastily. It took Aarav and Kabir almost ten minutes to pry them off without making too much noise. Once inside, a musty, moldy smell struck them like a wave. The corridor was narrow, lined with peeling wallpaper and rusted doors. At the end was a door with the number: **115**.

Vivaan's scanner began blinking faster.

"There's something definitely behind this door," he whispered.

Kiara took a deep breath and turned the knob.

The door opened with a slow, heavy creak.

Room 115: A Tomb of Secrets

Inside, Room 115 looked untouched by time. Dust floated in the air like ash. Child-size beds lined the walls—four of them. Rusted IV stands beside each bed. Notes pinned to a noticeboard bore strange symbols, formulas, and incomplete reports. Vivaan went straight to them.

"These notes… they're monitoring sleep cycles, stress levels, even… brainwave patterns. All from kids."

Meher walked slowly towards the far wall. A large, blacked-out mirror hung there. Beneath it, a drawing.

"Myra's drawing again…" she whispered. "A girl crying… with wires coming out of her head."

A loud **clunk** echoed behind them.

They turned. The door had shut on its own.

Kabir rushed to open it. It wouldn't budge.

And then… the lights flickered.

The Terror Awakens

Meher suddenly gasped. Her eyes rolled upward, and she collapsed. Aarav caught her before she hit the floor.

"Meher!" he shouted.

She wasn't unconscious. She was whispering something, over and over.

"It wasn't supposed to be like this… He watches… He punishes…"

Vivaan checked her pulse—it was racing.

Then, they heard it.

A scratching sound from inside the walls.

Kiara turned toward the mirror. Her breath caught in her throat.

Something moved behind it.

The glass wasn't a mirror—it was **one-way glass**, hiding an observation room.

A shadow stood on the other side.

No face. No form. Just darkness in the shape of a man.

The scratching grew louder.

Vivaan's scanner beeped furiously and suddenly shut off.

More Clues, More Questions

Kiara pulled open a metal drawer beneath one of the beds. Inside were syringes, labeled:

"PF-7X – Experimental Batch 3 (Unstable)"

And a photo. Myra, smiling weakly, sitting in the same room they were now in.

A chilling line was written on the back in child's handwriting:

"They said I'll become special. But I feel like I'm dying."

Tears welled in Kiara's eyes. "She trusted them…"

Suddenly, a projector in the ceiling turned on by itself. A flickering video played on the far wall. Footage of children in hospital gowns. Myra among them.

Then static.

Then, a scream.

Then, blackness.

The Unknown Ghost Strikes

Without warning, the walls began to shake. Books fell. The window shattered. From behind the mirror, **something began banging**—louder and louder.

Kabir screamed, "It's trying to come through!"

A whisper ran through the room, like wind but with words.

"You. Don't. Belong. Here."

The mirror cracked.

Meher suddenly sat up, eyes glowing faintly. Her voice changed.

"Run… it's not like the others. It doesn't want justice. It wants silence…"

The mirror shattered completely.

The faceless ghost stepped in.

It didn't float. It walked—slow, certain, filled with hatred.

Kiara screamed, "Everyone out!"

They grabbed Meher, kicked open the back wall and escaped through a maintenance hatch.

As they tumbled into the corridor, the sound of the thing howling filled the orphanage.

They didn't stop running.

The Aftermath

Back in their dormitory, Kiara locked the door and slumped against it. Her hands shook. Her heart pounded.

"We are in this now," she said. "There's no turning back."

Kabir collapsed onto the bed. "It doesn't want us to find the truth. That's why it's here."

Vivaan held up the blood-stained photo. "But the truth is already speaking. Myra… she still wants to be heard."

Meher lay silently, eyes open, still dazed.

And outside, beyond the dorm window, the orphanage stood silent once again.

But Room 115 was no longer just a place.

It was awake.

End of Chapter 6

7

The Journalist's Revelation

The air in the orphanage felt heavier than ever. It was like the building itself had started breathing—slow, cold, and suffocating. Meher kept whispering prayers under her breath, holding her locket tight. Vivaan hadn't slept for two nights; his biological scanner kept flashing unknown signals every few minutes.

Suddenly, Kiara's phone buzzed again.

This time, it rang only once before disconnecting.

Then a message appeared:

"Meet me before it's too late. — I.S."

No number. No ID.

Kiara's heartbeat quickened. "It's her... Isha Sen. The journalist."

"Are you sure?" Aarav asked.

Kiara nodded. "She knows something. Something big."

The Mysterious Meeting

They reached the old church on the outskirts of the village, half-ruined and buried in mist. A small tea stall stood nearby.

Behind it sat a woman wrapped in a dull shawl, eyes tired yet alert—**Isha Sen**.

She looked around nervously and waved them over. "You brought the letter?"

Kiara nodded and handed it over.

"I've been waiting for this moment," Isha whispered. "Ever since Myra's spirit contacted me."

Kabir frowned. "Spirit contacted you?"

"Yes," Isha replied, "through a radio frequency. It began with static… then whispers… then her voice."

She opened a rusted metal box and played an old tape recorder.

A slow, crackling sound played first. Then a soft girl's voice echoed:

"He's still here… he watches… from behind the mirror."

Chills ran down everyone's spine. Meher covered her ears.

The Buried Past Comes Alive

Isha opened her worn-out file. Inside were newspaper clippings, black-and-white photos, and a worn diary.

"Look," she said. "Children went missing here. Not once— multiple times over the years. The police never filed a case. Proton Foundation had too much power."

One clipping read:

"Seven Children Disappear in a Month — No Trace Found."

Another:

"Private Foundation Receives Grant for Human Bioengineering Study."

Vivaan stared at the headline, stunned. "Bioengineering… with children?"

"Yes," Isha replied grimly. "They tested on orphans—injecting unstable genes, forcing brainwave manipulation, even trying to genetically erase fear from the brain."

"That's insane," Aarav muttered.

"They thought they could create 'the perfect child,'" Isha said, voice shaking. "But something went horribly wrong."

She turned the page.

A rough sketch showed Myra strapped to a metallic chair, eyes wide, wires running through her head and chest. Blood stains dotted the edges of the paper.

"She wasn't the only one," Isha continued. "But she was the first to die... and the first to return."

The Spirit No One Understands

Isha flipped to another page. A strange, shadow-like figure had been drawn repeatedly in the margins.

A head too long... arms that stretched... no face—only blackness.

"What is that?" Meher whispered.

"That's the one I fear the most," Isha answered. "It was born out of a failed experiment. Not a child... not human. The foundation never documented it. It wasn't a victim... it was a mistake."

"And now it guards the orphanage," Vivaan added slowly. "It's the reason why the spirits can't rest... and why the truth can't leave this place."

Isha looked at them with haunted eyes. "I call it *The Watcher*. It feeds on fear. And the more you discover, the more it attacks."

Dark Phenomena Begin Again

Back in the orphanage, their return triggered something evil.

- A broken tape recorder began spinning by itself and whispered in a cracked voice:
- **"Stop digging. Truth must rot."**
- Vivaan's device began flashing violently every time they passed by the old hallway.
- A painting of a tree in the corridor melted into a dark, writhing face that screamed before fading into the wall.
- Meher fell to the ground during dinner, her eyes rolled back, and she began speaking in Myra's voice:
- **"He lives... behind Room 115... under the floor."**

The group rushed to her aid. It took nearly ten minutes to wake her up.

Another Message from Myra

That night, Kiara had another dream.

Myra stood at the end of a long hallway, crying. Her face was pale and stitched at the mouth. When she reached out her hand, blood ran from her eyes.

"Set me free... before he silences me forever."

Kiara woke with a gasp, her pillow soaked in sweat.

On the wall above her bed, written in red:

"Truth dies if spoken."

The letters began to melt and vanish before her eyes.

A Dangerous Lead

Isha told them about Saraswati Didi—the only person alive who worked at the orphanage during the experiments.

"She lives far from here now. In hiding. She's the last key."

"Then we go to her," Kiara said, voice firm. "We've come too far to stop now."

But outside the orphanage, something moved in the shadows… something tall… formless… watching.

As they packed to leave, every window in the orphanage cracked—at once.

A deep, growling whisper filled the halls:

"You bring light to what must remain dark."

And then silence.

But the threat was now clear—*The Watcher* knew.

End of Chapter 7

8

The Caretaker's Tale

The cracked windows still trembled in their frames. Kiara stood frozen, staring into the darkness beyond the glass. That voice—the growl that came from nowhere—still echoed in her mind.

"You bring light to what must remain dark."

The group didn't speak for a while. It was as if the orphanage itself was warning them… or begging them to stop.

Vivaan slowly turned off his device. The scanner's red light flickered one last time and died. "It drained the battery," he whispered. "That… thing. It's not just a spirit."

Aarav looked outside. "We leave at first light. Isha gave us her address. Saraswati Didi is the only one left who knows the full truth."

They left in silence the next morning, the orphanage watching them like a predator waiting for its prey to return.

A Journey into the Forgotten Hills

Saraswati Didi lived far from the village, deep in the hills, in a fading cottage covered with moss. The trees here were older…

darker. The silence was thick, broken only by the crunching of dry leaves underfoot.

When they knocked on the cottage door, it didn't open.

Meher whispered, "What if she's already—"

Before she could finish, the door creaked open. A wrinkled woman with silver hair and a bent back stood there, her eyes sharp and wide.

"I told her this day would come," she said softly, her voice like the rustling of old paper. "Come in."

The Cottage of Secrets

Inside, the cottage was filled with small statues, burning incense, and thick bundles of dried herbs. A large photo of Goddess Kali hung above the fireplace. It smelled like old books and wet stone.

Saraswati Didi offered them all tea. "You've seen them, haven't you? The children. Especially the one with the stitched lips."

"Yes," Kiara said. "Myra."

Saraswati sighed. Her hands trembled slightly as she lifted a heavy iron box from under the floorboard.

"I was there," she said. "I took care of them—fed them, cleaned their wounds, sang them to sleep. Until... until the science people came."

The Experiments Begin

"Proton Foundation," she spat the name. "They promised to build a better future. Said they would give orphans a 'gifted mind.' What they really wanted... was to change what it means to be human."

Everyone leaned forward. Vivaan took out his notebook.

"They gave injections—strange glowing liquids. Children were strapped into machines. Some screamed for hours. Others… just sat still and smiled like dolls. And Myra… she was the strongest. But her body couldn't hold the changes."

"What kind of changes?" Vivaan asked.

"They tried to alter the fear center in the brain," she replied. "Make the children brave beyond nature. They used synthetic neurotransmitters. But the dose was too high. The brain stopped reacting to pain. And the body… started breaking."

She pulled out an old photo of Myra—eyes wide, wires in her head, blood at the nose.

"She didn't scream when her bones snapped. She just cried. Quietly. Every night."

Everyone went silent. Aarav clenched his fists. Meher wiped her eyes.

"And then," Saraswati whispered, "she died. But she didn't leave."

The Unknown Ghost Appears

"But Myra isn't the one you should be afraid of," Saraswati continued. Her voice shook now. "There's another. One that was never born… only created."

Kiara looked up sharply. "The Watcher?"

Saraswati nodded. "Yes. The failed result of their worst experiment. It was a merging of different brain patterns—a test tube brain, grown from brain tissues of dead criminals, and reprogrammed with artificial instincts. No soul. No memory. Only hunger."

"They called it a success," she continued. "But it escaped… killed three doctors and vanished into the old forest. The orphanage was sealed for a year. When it reopened, strange things started happening."

Meher whispered, "So it's not a ghost?"

"It's worse," Saraswati said. "It was never alive… so it can't be killed. It exists between realms—feeding off fear, corrupting minds. It guards Room 115."

The Bloody Room

Vivaan pulled out his old blueprint of the orphanage. "Room 115 was never on the original map."

"Because it was built secretly," Saraswati said. "Underground. A testing chamber where Myra died. A place where *he* still lives."

"I need to go there," Kiara said suddenly.

"Are you mad?" Kabir snapped. "You've seen what it does to people!"

"She's right," Aarav said quietly. "This has to end. And it ends in that room."

Saraswati stood and slowly opened a rusted drawer. She handed Kiara a tiny metal key. "This opens the trapdoor under the staircase. The path to Room 115 begins there."

"But beware," she added, looking at each of them. "Once you open that path… it can never be closed again."

A Final Warning

As they were about to leave, Saraswati held Kiara's hand tightly.

"Myra has waited for justice. But *he* has waited for silence. If you fail, he'll bury your truth with you."

"Then we won't fail," Kiara whispered. "We promise."

Outside, the clouds darkened. Thunder rolled over the hills. The road back to the orphanage felt longer. Every step heavier.

Vivaan stared at the blueprint again.

"Next stop," he said, voice grim, "Room 115."

And somewhere far away, a shadow moved across a mirror inside the orphanage.

It had no eyes.

But it was watching.

End of Chapter 8

9

The Underground Chamber

The sun had long disappeared behind the clouds as the group stood frozen outside the narrow staircase that led beneath the orphanage floor. The air had grown heavier, as if the orphanage itself didn't want them to go any further.

Saraswati Didi's story still echoed in their minds. Myra's death wasn't just a tragedy—it was a result of a failed bio-experiment, a brutal reality wrapped in scientific madness. The clues were no longer scattered—they were aligning, and the source seemed buried somewhere below their feet.

Aarav stepped forward first, his flashlight trembling in his hand. "We've come this far. We have to know the whole truth," he said, his voice low but firm.

The Descent Begins

The stairs creaked under their weight. With every step downward, the light from above dimmed, swallowed by the thick darkness around them. The walls were moist, covered with strange moss-like growths. A foul stench of rotten chemicals mixed with decaying flesh filled the air.

Vivaan, holding his bio-detection device, noticed something.

"The radiation and temperature spikes are higher here," he whispered, pointing at the screen. "It's definitely not a normal basement."

The stairs ended in a large metallic door—rusted, locked with chains and bolts. Kiara searched around and found an old locker in the corner. Inside was a rusted key, almost like fate had left it behind.

The Forgotten Laboratory

With a screech, the door creaked open. The chamber inside was not a basement—it was a full-blown laboratory.

Broken machines, shattered tubes, surgical tables, and empty cages lined the walls. On one table lay a tattered file labeled **"Project Purity – Subject M.V."**

Kiara picked it up carefully. Inside were horrifying details.

"Subject: Myra Verma – Female, Age 10. Selected for Stage IV Neural-Stem Infusion. Rejected by body. Neurological seizure followed by cardiac collapse. Cause of death: Bio-systemic failure. Mark: Classified."

Vivaan's hands shook as he translated the file.

"They tried injecting her with genetically engineered stem cells designed to 'purify' emotional aggression. They were trying to create emotionless, obedient children…"

"But why her?" Meher whispered, horrified.

Kabir pointed to a monitor near the corner. "She was emotionally strong. They wanted to erase her emotions."

The Ghost Appears

Suddenly, the lights flickered. A low humming filled the room. The temperature dropped sharply.

The air turned heavy.

And then—Myra appeared.

But this time, her form was more than just shadow. She looked part-real, part-illusion, glowing with a ghostly white light. Her eyes weren't angry... they were filled with pain.

"You found it..." her voice echoed. "Now you must finish it."

Before anyone could speak, the lights burst, plunging the lab into total darkness.

Blood on the Walls

In the torchlight, they saw writing appear on the wall—written in what looked like fresh blood:

"STOP HIM."

"Stop who?" Kabir muttered, backing away.

The door behind them slammed shut on its own.

The Trap

From the ceiling, a recording device clicked on.

A distorted voice played through the speakers—it was Dr. Radhika Kapoor, head of the Proton Foundation.

"We created life in our own image... but the test subjects were unstable. Subject M.V. escaped neural control. She infected others. The chamber must remain sealed. No one must know..."

Suddenly, Vivaan's device beeped wildly. A hidden door in the wall creaked open. Behind it was a tunnel.

The Unknown Entity Strikes

Just as they turned, the unknown ghost—**the one not tied to any child, the one not a victim**—emerged from the shadows. It didn't look human. Its form kept shifting, and its scream shattered glass nearby.

It attacked violently.

Kabir was thrown against the wall, bleeding from his forehead. Meher screamed, frozen in place. The creature wasn't bound by emotion—it radiated pure chaos.

"RUN!" Kiara shouted, pulling Meher with her.

They fled into the tunnel, narrowly avoiding another attack. The ghost didn't follow them. It stopped at the lab's edge… as if trapped within.

Vivaan gasped, "That thing… it's guarding the lab. It doesn't want the truth to come out."

The Tunnel's Secret

The tunnel stretched for hundreds of meters. Along the walls were scratched drawings—by children, perhaps by Myra herself. They showed the truth—kids crying, tubes in arms, doctors watching without care. One picture showed Myra inside a large tank—screaming.

At the end of the tunnel was another metal gate. This one had a keypad.

Aarav remembered something—Myra's birthday, seen earlier on a medical file: 11/05.

He punched in 1105.

The gate opened.

They stepped into another room. Unlike the lab, this room looked like a child's room—clean, untouched. On the wall was a single sentence:

"I wasn't alone."

The room shook.

The ground beneath them cracked.

A Lift to the Final Truth

In the center of the room was a lift—old, rusted, but still working. It had a button marked **"Sub-Zero – Restricted"**.

They looked at each other.

"What's worse than all we've seen?" Kabir whispered.

"We're about to find out," Kiara replied.

As the lift descended into darkness, they knew this was no longer just a haunted orphanage. It was a war between hidden truths and supernatural horrors—between science gone wrong and spirits that refused to be forgotten.

The real story… was just beginning.

End of Chapter 9

10

The Experiment Room

The metallic doors of the **Sub-Zero – Restricted** lift groaned as they opened. A cold gust of air escaped, chilling the group to their bones. A thin layer of frost clung to the walls inside the shaft, and the dim blue emergency lights inside flickered irregularly, casting eerie shadows on their anxious faces.

"No turning back now," whispered Kiara, her voice steady but low.

Vivaan checked the screen on his biological detection device—it was blinking red with strange frequency pulses. "This is beyond any radiation or biological field I've ever studied," he muttered, worried. "There's something… wrong down there. Alive, maybe. But… not natural."

Still, the group stepped inside. The lift jerked once and then began its slow descent.

Sub-Level 1… Sub-Level 2… Sub-Level 3…

When it stopped at Sub-Level 5, the doors creaked open. A heavy darkness loomed ahead. No lights. No sounds. Just a stale, chemical odor.

"Flashlights," Aarav whispered. The students switched them

on.

Before them lay a wide underground corridor lined with rusted metallic walls. The air felt sterile, but beneath it was something foul—a mix of decayed matter and synthetic chemicals.

They walked cautiously, passing sealed glass rooms. Some held rusted operating tables, broken surgical lights, and shattered beakers. Others displayed child-sized chairs fixed with restraining belts. Blood stains, faded and dry, marked the walls like forgotten memories.

Suddenly, a loud **thud** echoed behind them. They turned—but nothing. Only shadows.

"Did you hear that?" Meher whispered.

A door up ahead blinked red with a sign: **Experiment Chamber – X113: Access Restricted.**

Vivaan approached the keypad. "It's locked, but maybe…"

Isha Sen stepped forward. "Wait. I think I have something." She pulled out a small USB stick from her bag. "I got it from Dr. Rathod's lab—he didn't know I took it."

She inserted it into the emergency override panel. After a few seconds, the door hissed open.

Inside was a massive room, circular in shape, with a domed ceiling and faded murals on the wall—murals of children smiling, holding flowers, and playing. It was a deception. A lie.

In the center stood a large, sealed glass chamber with what looked like **suspended gel** inside. Tubes ran in and out of it, and floating within the gel was a child's skeleton—small, delicate, and horrifying.

On the floor around the chamber were discarded files, broken tablets, and shattered syringes.

Vivaan picked up a folder marked: **"Project: Cell Enhance-**

ment – Prototype Myra Verma."

He read aloud:

"Subject shows extreme emotional resistance. Synthetic virus injection at Stage 2 caused unexpected neural response. Subject experienced intense pain, seizures, and eventually… silence. Possible cerebral collapse. Cause of death: pending investigation."

The group stood in silence.

Tears welled up in Meher's eyes. "She was just a little girl…"

Suddenly, the lights flickered. A long, high-pitched whisper echoed through the room.

Aarav turned quickly. "Did you hear that?"

They looked toward the wall behind the chamber. A dark smudge was spreading, as if the very concrete was bleeding.

Then it happened.

A projector screen mounted above flickered to life. Footage began playing—a young Myra strapped to a bed, screaming, thrashing, begging. Scientists in white coats stood over her. One of them was clearly **Dr. Radhika Kapoor**.

"Increase the voltage," Radhika ordered.

"Her brainwave activity is destabilizing," another scientist warned.

"She must adapt. We need the reaction," Radhika insisted coldly.

The screen suddenly cracked and burst into static.

Meher collapsed to her knees, possessed by a wave of emotions. She held her head, eyes wide. "She's here… she's crying… she doesn't want to be alone…"

Suddenly, a loud **crash**. The Unknown Ghost appeared—tall, distorted, faceless—its mouth stretching unnaturally wide as if screaming, but no sound came.

It rushed forward.

Kiara pulled Meher up and shouted, "Run!"

The group bolted through the other door on the far end. They ran into another hallway—this one narrower, with walls covered in **notes, drawings,** and **blood prints.**

Vivaan paused to read one:

"They lied to us. We were their lab rats. I want my mother."

"My name is Raghav. I hurt. I die. I return."

And beneath it: **"You are not supposed to be here."**

"Guys…" Vivaan pointed. "This wasn't just one experiment. There were more. Many more."

Kabir shook his head. "No wonder they tried to bury this place."

Suddenly, Aarav noticed a black journal lying next to a torn lab coat.

Inside were the final notes of Dr. Rajiv Malhotra.

"We tried to replicate cell regeneration using synthetic viral proteins combined with CRISPR-type gene editing. But the emotional trauma in children caused neurological side effects. One child's brain cells mutated so fast, it created a psychic backlash. I think she's still here… somewhere."

As they turned the page, a single line sent chills down their spine:

"If the truth ever comes out, the world will know: We created our own monster."

End of Chapter 10

11

The Escape Plan

The moment they closed the door behind them, Aarav locked it with a rusted rod he found lying near the wall. His breath was heavy, heart pounding as if it would jump out of his chest.

"What was that *thing*?" Kabir gasped, wiping the sweat from his forehead. "It wasn't Myra or Raghav... it felt different. Darker. Violent."

"I don't think it wants to protect anything," Meher murmured. "It wants to destroy. It doesn't care who we are."

They had entered a smaller maintenance room, filled with scattered tools, broken monitors, and old blueprints of the building. The walls were cracked, and mold clung to every surface. A single red emergency light blinked weakly overhead.

Vivaan flipped through one of the blueprint scrolls. "Look. This chamber we're in now—there's a hidden exit that leads toward the old storm drain beneath the hill. It was used for chemical waste disposal. If it's still open... we can escape."

Kiara frowned. "That's if we survive the path."

Just then, the lights buzzed and went out. Complete blackness surrounded them for a moment. And in that darkness... a whisper.

Not loud.

Just near their ears, like breath brushing against skin.

"You're not leaving…"

Meher clutched Kiara's arm. Her eyes rolled back for a second before she gasped, "It's not just one ghost… it's many. All the children… and that other thing… it *feeds* on their pain."

Kabir swung his flashlight around. "We need to move. Now."

They followed the map Vivaan marked, creeping through narrow corridors, stepping over broken wires and rusted pipes. With every step, the air grew heavier—more pungent, more toxic. Vivaan held a handkerchief to his mouth. "This section hasn't been ventilated for years."

Suddenly, they reached a heavy, rusted hatch labeled:

"Hazard Zone: Disposal Access – Entry Forbidden"

Aarav twisted the valve with all his strength. It groaned, metal screeching against metal, and finally creaked open. A rush of warm, stale air hit them.

They stepped inside.

The space looked like an old processing unit. Rotating drums, broken incinerators, and thick chemical pipes surrounded them. On the far wall was a large steel duct leading downward.

"That's the way," Vivaan confirmed.

But before they could move, the **Unknown Ghost** appeared again—this time at the entrance behind them, blocking their way back.

It shrieked—a horrible, echoing screech like metal tearing through bone. Lights exploded above them. Sparks flew. Kabir slipped and fell as the ghost lunged forward with unearthly speed.

"Go!" Aarav screamed, pulling Kabir to his feet.

They ran toward the duct. But suddenly, the duct door **slammed shut**—on its own.

Trapped.

Kiara frantically looked around. "There has to be another way!"

Meher suddenly screamed—not in fear, but in *pain*. Her body twisted unnaturally as she pointed toward a small access tunnel near the ceiling. "There—go!"

Aarav climbed a pipe and kicked the loose panel open. "Come on, one at a time!"

One by one, they helped each other up. Vivaan went last, pulling Meher with him, who was shivering violently.

As they crawled through the tight space, the ghost below screeched again, shaking the entire vent. Walls cracked. The air thinned.

Kabir coughed hard. "We're not going to make it—"

"Yes, we are!" Kiara snapped. "We didn't come this far to die here!"

Finally, they slid out into a smaller corridor. A sign on the wall read:

"Outflow Tunnel – To Drainage Exit"

But what they saw next stopped them cold.

In front of the drainage gate lay the half-burned body of a man. On his chest, scorched into the skin, was a word:

"TRAITOR"

Vivaan knelt beside him and found a half-melted ID tag.

Dr. Rajiv Malhotra.

"He tried to run," Vivaan whispered. "The ghost… it caught him."

Kiara looked at the gate. "We have to keep moving."

Aarav found a manual crank. With effort, he turned it—and

the metal gate slowly lifted, revealing a long, sloped tunnel leading outside.

As they stepped into the tunnel, the ground behind them shook. Cries. Screams. Child voices mixed with sobs. And one angry voice rising above them all.

The Unknown Ghost was coming.

They ran, sliding down the wet concrete slope. The wind howled behind them. The light ahead grew brighter.

They emerged into the open—the base of the hill behind the orphanage, under the moonlight. But none of them felt relief.

Not yet.

Because as they turned back to look at the building from a distance…

They saw **someone watching them** from the top floor window.

A shadow.

Still.

Silent.

And then, as if mocking them, **the lights inside Room 115 flickered on.**

Meher fainted.

Aarav caught her. "We made it out… but it's not over."

Vivaan stared at the flickering light. "The truth hasn't left. Not yet."

End of Chapter 11

12

The Curse Unveiled

The night was quiet—too quiet.

The group stood at the base of the hill, eyes fixed on the orphanage. The flickering light in Room 115 continued to glow like a warning. Meher lay unconscious, her body trembling. Aarav held her protectively while the others gathered around, panting, bruised, and haunted.

"We're out…" Kabir whispered. "But it doesn't feel like we are."

Kiara knelt beside Meher and gently tapped her cheek. "Meher… please wake up…"

Vivaan checked her pulse. "She's alive… but something's wrong. Her mind—it's stuck."

Suddenly, Meher jolted awake with a scream. *"They won't let us leave!* They said we belong to the orphanage now!"

Everyone froze.

Meher's voice was different—low and trembling, like someone else was speaking through her.

"They all died… *not by accident,*" she whispered. "The curse began… the moment the foundation broke its promise…"

"What promise?" Aarav asked softly, kneeling beside her.

Meher's eyes rolled back, and in that cold, empty voice, she continued:

"They were supposed to heal us… but they turned us into monsters. Every scream, every injection, every failed experiment… sealed the curse into the bones of that place."

And then, silence.

She passed out again.

Kabir looked pale. "Are you saying the curse was created because of the experiments?"

Vivaan nodded slowly. "Yes. Remember what Dr. Rathod said—the biological trials weren't just failures. They were crimes against nature. They altered the children's DNA. Many of them died in agony."

"And Myra?" Kiara asked. "She was the start?"

Vivaan looked up. "No. She was the spark. But the curse… it's older. Deeper. Maybe even… planted."

A sudden realization hit Aarav. "The Unknown Ghost. It doesn't want revenge. It wants silence. It attacks anyone who tries to reveal the truth."

Kabir added, "Like a guard. Or… a *punisher.* It's bound to the curse."

Just then, they heard rustling in the nearby trees.

They turned—on edge.

A frail figure stepped out of the woods—**Saraswati Didi.**

She looked shaken, but unharmed. "I saw the lights from the hill. I knew… you went inside."

Kiara rushed to her. "We found everything. The lab. The spirits. The truth. But there's more, isn't there?"

Saraswati nodded slowly, tears in her eyes.

"You need to understand… curses are not magic. They are

energy—pain, betrayal, suffering—all fused into one place. That building… the orphanage… it *remembers.* And it holds every scream like blood stains in its walls."

"Who created it?" Aarav asked. "The curse."

"I don't know who… but I know why."

She sat on a stone and took a shaky breath.

"They promised to create cures. They brought us hope. Then they started locking children away. The doctors changed. The warden became cruel. The floors below—full of screams we couldn't reach. One night… everything went silent. And from that night, Room 115… changed."

Vivaan pulled out a notebook he took from the lab. "There's a final page here. It mentions something called '**The Binding Ritual**'. It says: *Failure to complete it will trap the anomaly within the site.*"

"The anomaly?" Kabir asked.

Saraswati Didi closed her eyes. "The Unknown Ghost."

Everyone fell silent.

Meher stirred again. Her voice returned, weak but clear. "It can't be stopped. It was born from all of them. Their pain. Their rage. And the curse… lives through it."

Aarav looked at the orphanage in the distance.

"Then we don't just need to escape," he said, voice firm. "We need to end the curse."

"But how?" Kiara asked.

Vivaan opened the notebook again. "There's one last clue. The ritual was never finished because one person…*disappeared.*"

Kabir leaned in. "Who?"

Vivaan pointed to the name at the bottom of the page:

Dr. Radhika Kapoor.

Kiara's eyes widened. "She's alive?"

Saraswati nodded slowly. "If she is… she's the last one who knows how to stop it."

Aarav stood up. "Then we find her."

A strong wind howled through the trees. Room 115's light flickered once more—and then went dark.

As if it had heard their decision.

As if it was… waiting.

End of Chapter 12

13

The Final Scientist

A New Lead

The morning sun was dull behind thick clouds, as if even the sky mourned the secrets buried in the orphanage.

The group gathered at Saraswati Didi's house. A new fire burned in their eyes. They had escaped once—but now, they were going back in. Not out of fear, but for closure.

Vivaan spread out his notes on the table. "The last known scientist involved in the experiments was Dr. Radhika Kapoor. She disappeared after the lab was sealed. No reports. No trace."

"Do you think she's dead?" Meher asked softly.

Saraswati shook her head. "She was different. Cold…focused. But she feared something in the end. She left without a word."

"We have to find her," Aarav said. "She may be the only one who can reverse this… or explain what truly happened."

Tracking the Scientist

Kiara contacted Isha Sen, the journalist, who had access to old Proton Foundation employee records. A few hours later, Isha returned with a file.

"Dr. Radhika Kapoor moved to a secluded village years ago. Changed her name—Rekha Varma. Lives in an isolated estate near the outskirts of Koti village."

"That's two hours from here," Kabir said, checking the map. "But the road ends near a forest."

Aarav nodded. "We've gone through worse. Let's find her."

The Isolated Estate

By evening, the group reached the edge of Koti village. The locals avoided the forest trail ahead.

"She doesn't come out," an old villager warned. "No visitors. No phone. But sometimes, we hear… screams."

The estate loomed like a haunted fortress—overgrown with vines, broken fences, and a silence that screamed suspicion. They pushed open the rusted gate and entered.

The house was locked, but Vivaan noticed a surveillance camera—functional.

"She knows we're here," he whispered.

A voice echoed from a speaker above the door. "Leave."

Aarav stepped forward. "Dr. Kapoor—we know what you did. But we need answers. People died. And something is still alive inside the orphanage."

Silence.

Then—click—the door opened.

Confronting the Truth

Dr. Radhika Kapoor looked nothing like a monster. Her face was tired, aged beyond her years. Her eyes, however, carried guilt and fear.

"You shouldn't have come," she said.

"You created the curse," Kiara said. "Didn't you?"

"No," Radhika whispered. "I created the science. But the curse... it was a consequence. Something we didn't understand."

Vivaan stepped forward. "Tell us everything."

Radhika looked down. "The Proton Foundation's goal was to build genetic resistance against illness—cure immunity failures. We used orphan children... because they had no guardians. No one to question us."

"And Myra?" Meher asked, her voice shaking.

"Myra was Subject Zero-One-Five. She showed signs of psychic response—dream-linked memory, unnatural perception. When we tried to suppress those traits... she died in agony."

The room went cold.

"She didn't die alone," Radhika continued. "Something... was released from her. A psychic storm. It affected the other children. Many died. Others changed. One of them... became the *Anomaly*."

"The Unknown Ghost," Kabir whispered.

Radhika nodded. "It wasn't a ghost at first. It was a *force*. But when trapped, it needed a vessel. And it found one."

The Binding Ritual

"There was a plan," Radhika said, walking to an old cabinet. She pulled out a hidden file titled: *Binding Protocol — Project Delta-Black*.

She opened it.

"The ritual wasn't religious. It was scientific. We had to neutralize the anomaly's psychic frequency by syncing it with its origin—Myra's DNA. But her body was gone... burned during the escape."

"So the ritual failed," Vivaan realized.

"Yes," she whispered. "And the anomaly became unstable.

It no longer wanted revenge. It wanted isolation. It silenced everyone who tried to reveal the truth."

"So what now?" Kiara asked.

Radhika handed them the final page.

"There's a backup plan. If Myra's remains—or her energy signature—can be recovered, we can trap the anomaly in one final containment. But it has to be done *inside* Room 115."

The group stared at the page. It detailed a scientific-device-assisted binding using heatwaves, resonance pulses, and memory-stimulation triggers. It could work. But it was dangerous.

The Final Choice

"You have a choice," Radhika said. "Run. Leave it be. Or go back and seal the curse forever."

Aarav clenched his fists. "Too many people have died. This ends with us."

Kiara looked at the others. Each one of them nodded.

"We go back," she said. "One last time."

A thunderstorm rumbled in the distance, as if the orphanage had heard them… and was waiting.

End of Chapter 13

14

Back to Room 115

The Return Begins

The journey back to the orphanage was silent. The roads felt darker than before, as if nature itself was aware of their mission. The wind whispered like voices, and trees swayed with eerie movements.

They were not just returning to a haunted building—they were stepping into a battlefield where science, guilt, revenge, and the unknown collided.

Vivaan double-checked the equipment: the portable heat generator, the resonance pulse module, memory activators, and the specially developed containment device designed from Dr. Kapoor's files.

"This time, we don't run," Aarav said firmly.

"No matter what we see," Kiara added, "we finish it."

Preparing the Final Setup

The team entered through the back gate. Inside, the walls seemed even more decayed, and the air heavier than before. The sound of water dripping echoed like ticking time.

They headed straight toward Room 115.

Vivaan began installing the pulse-emitter near the corner of the room. Its purpose: to awaken any remaining psychic residue left by Myra.

Meher placed candles and resonance beads at each corner—objects Myra was emotionally connected to, meant to trigger her emotional presence.

Aarav wired the heat generator to the containment device, as the ritual called for a balance of emotional connection and scientific resonance.

"Time is short," Kabir whispered. "We must trigger the memory sequence... now."

The Ritual Begins

Kiara took out Myra's old drawing, which they had retrieved earlier. She placed it in the center of the room. A faint gust blew through the sealed room.

Meher began speaking softly, as if calling out: "Myra... you were never forgotten. We're here to help you. Let go of the pain..."

Suddenly, the drawing began to twitch. Not move—*twitch*. As if something behind the paper was breathing.

Vivaan started the resonance pulse. The room began to hum with low frequency waves. A faint golden glow appeared on the floor beneath Myra's drawing.

Then the temperature dropped.

The Unknown Ghost Attacks

Before anyone could react, the lights burst. A sudden black mist filled the room. The walls bled again—this time faster, the words forming: **"YOU CANNOT FREE THE TRUTH."**

A deep, distorted growl shook the air. The Unknown Ghost appeared—not as a child, not as Myra—but as a twisted figure of burnt flesh, hollow eyes, and a permanently screaming mouth. It was monstrous and unnatural, its presence more psychic than physical.

It charged toward Meher—but this time, Meher didn't run. She stood, whispering the binding chant Dr. Kapoor had taught them.

Vivaan triggered the memory stimulator.

The Final Confrontation

Myra's spirit appeared—glowing faintly in the golden light from the resonance pulses. She looked scared but peaceful.

"Myra," Kiara called, her voice trembling, "You have to help us. This… thing, it's not you. But only you can stop it!"

The Unknown Ghost screamed and surged forward. As it did, Myra raised her hand. Light clashed with shadow. The resonance pulse shook violently.

Vivaan increased the heat signal.

The shadow was weakening—but not enough.

Dr. Kapoor's voice rang in Aarav's memory: *"Only when the subject accepts its pain... can the anomaly be weakened."*

Aarav stepped forward, holding Myra's photo from the journal.

"Myra, it wasn't your fault. We're sorry for what they did. But you don't have to carry this alone."

Containment

Myra's spirit turned to the Unknown Ghost.

"No more," she whispered.

A scream echoed, not from the ghost—but from the *orphanage itself.* The floor cracked, walls bled dark matter, and wind howled as if a thousand trapped voices were being released.

Vivaan initiated the containment.

The ghost was pulled toward the device—fighting, screeching, leaving claw marks in the air—but it had no choice.

As it was sucked inside, a loud **bang** echoed, and then—silence.

The lights flickered back. The golden glow faded.

Myra was gone. The room was quiet.

Aftermath

The group collapsed on the floor, exhausted, eyes wide in disbelief.

"It's… over?" Kabir whispered.

The resonance device showed no anomaly.

Kiara walked to the center of the room, where Myra's drawing still lay. Only now, the figure had changed—it was a smiling girl with wings.

"She's free," Meher said softly.

A New Dawn

They stepped out of the orphanage just as the first sunlight pierced the horizon. The birds sang. The forest no longer felt cursed.

Though the building remained, its evil had been sealed—maybe not forever, but long enough for peace to return.

They had survived. They had uncovered the truth.

And they had freed a lost soul.

End of Chapter 14

15

Truth and Trial

The Silent Ride Back

The group sat quietly in the van as they drove back to the city. No one spoke.

Aarav stared out the window, watching the trees pass by, each one reminding him of the nightmare they'd survived. Kiara clutched the old photograph of Myra. Kabir kept his eyes closed, breathing slowly as if trying to hold his emotions inside. Meher held her spiritual beads, occasionally whispering prayers. Vivaan, with bloodshot eyes, kept glancing at his equipment — all readings stable. No anomalies.

But deep inside, they all knew — this was far from over.

Return to the Real World

As the city lights returned, reality hit them like a wave.

News of their disappearance had spread. Isha Sen's final article had been scheduled for automatic release if she didn't return in 48 hours. The media had exploded with curiosity: *"Haunted Orphanage Mystery — Students Missing During Investigation."*

They had to explain everything — carefully.

But how do you explain the supernatural, biological experiments, and spirits… and still be believed?

The Government's Involvement

Soon after their return, they were summoned by a secret government division. Officials had intercepted Isha's files, especially the ones involving Proton Foundation.

A man in a black coat with no visible ID said to Aarav and Kiara during questioning, "We have reason to believe what you uncovered goes beyond that orphanage. The Proton Foundation was only one node in a larger web."

They tried to keep the group separated, asking each of them questions individually. Some believed them. Some laughed. Some… seemed scared.

What they didn't know was that the device Vivaan used to contain the Unknown Ghost had been quietly secured by Dr. Rathod, who had gone off-grid.

The Legal Battle Begins

Isha Sen returned to her newsroom and bravely published a series of articles with all the evidence she had. Photos of the lab, the underground chamber, testimonies from Dr. Rathod, and Saraswati Didi's records.

Proton Foundation denied all accusations.

Their legal team declared:

"These are fabricated lies by trespassers and a runaway ex-employee. The orphanage was closed due to safety hazards — nothing more."

But the public was enraged. Children's lives had been lost. Myra's photo became the face of the movement. People demanded justice.

Threats and Shadows

Aarav and Kiara started receiving anonymous messages:

- *"Stop digging."*
- *"You don't know what you're messing with."*
- *"You freed something you can't contain."*

One evening, Kiara found her window marked with a familiar ritual symbol — the same that was behind the forbidden door in Chapter 4.

Was it a warning?

Was the Unknown Ghost truly contained?

Or… was something else watching?

Closure for Myra and Others

Meher led a small memorial for the lost children — especially Myra, Raghav, and Neha.

The forest surrounding the orphanage had turned peaceful. Birds chirped. The trees no longer whispered danger.

The villagers, once terrified, began rebuilding lives. But no one dared go near Room 115.

Kiara placed the drawing of the smiling Myra in a glass frame and gave it to Saraswati Didi.

"She's at peace now," she said.

Saraswati Didi simply nodded, tears in her eyes.

"Yes… but something else still roams."

The Final Revelation (Hint)

Vivaan met Aarav late one night, weeks later.

"I kept scanning the containment device," he said. "It's stable… but sometimes I hear whispers."

Aarav frowned. "You think the Unknown Ghost is… communicating?"

"No," Vivaan replied, his voice shaking. "It's *not just that ghost. There's another voice inside. One we never met.*"

Aarav's stomach dropped.

"Then… what did we trap?"

Vivaan looked at him.

"I don't know. But I don't think this was the end. I think it was just… a beginning."

End of Chapter 15

16

The Final Whisper

A Strange Signal

It was late evening. The sky was a deep red, and a cold breeze blew through Vivaan's apartment window. His devices began to blink suddenly—his biological scanner, which had been silent for weeks, was now reacting.

Low-frequency vibrations. Pulse readings. Unstable spikes.

Vivaan checked the coordinates the device was picking up. He froze.

It was pointing toward… **an abandoned medical facility**—once owned by Proton Foundation, located *far* from the orphanage.

Return of the Team

Vivaan immediately called Aarav, Kiara, Kabir, Meher, and Dr. Rathod. The team gathered at Kiara's home, still haunted by past trauma—but they all knew they couldn't ignore this.

"This place was off-limits even to us," Dr. Rathod explained. "Only top-level researchers had access. It was used for advanced experimental trials… more secretive than the orphanage."

"But what would the ghost want there?" Kabir asked.

"It's not just about the ghost anymore," Vivaan said. "It's about *what we missed.*"

The Journey to the Unknown Facility

The facility was buried deep in a forested area. Overgrown weeds covered rusted fences. The sign at the gate had been scratched beyond recognition, but the faded outline of the Proton Foundation logo remained.

The team entered through a side door—rusted but unlocked.

Inside, everything was quiet. Unnaturally quiet.

As they explored the dusty corridors, Kiara whispered, "This silence… it's like the building is *watching us.*"

The Hidden Archive Room

They found a hidden door behind a shelf in the administrative office. It led to a chamber filled with **old biological samples, dusty files, and video cassettes**.

Vivaan began examining the chemical labels—unfamiliar compounds mixed with human DNA markers.

Rathod read an old report aloud:

"Subject-X was created to suppress psychic consciousness. Designed to protect experiments from supernatural interference…"

Aarav's heart skipped. "Subject-X… is that the Unknown Ghost?"

Rathod nodded slowly, realization dawning. "It wasn't a victim… it was *created.*"

The Final Tape

They found a broken tape recorder—similar to the one they'd encountered before. Kabir managed to fix it using spare parts from Vivaan's toolkit.

The tape played, full of static… then a distorted voice:

"We thought we could control it. We were wrong. It speaks in dreams now. It is no longer confined to this world… It's evolving."

Suddenly, the room temperature dropped.

Meher fell to her knees, her eyes wide.

"She's here… and something else too."

The True Nature of the Unknown Ghost

In the lowest level of the facility, they discovered a bio-containment chamber marked: **PROJECT VOID**.

Inside was a **black stain on the wall**, burnt in the shape of a handprint.

Vivaan checked his scanner—it went completely haywire.

"No DNA. No thermal signature. It's as if this thing… isn't even alive."

Rathod stepped forward, his voice trembling.

"We created this entity from leftover spiritual energy, brain-wave manipulation, and failed consciousness experiments. Its purpose was to *block spirits*, keep test sites hidden."

"But it gained awareness," Kiara said, horrified.

"It knew what it was… and it turned."

The Last Stand

Suddenly, the lights burst.

A loud, screeching sound echoed in the halls. The doors slammed shut. Darkness swallowed the room.

The entity—black, formless, and massive—emerged from the shadows. It **wasn't Myra**. It was **something darker**.

The ghost screamed with rage, blasting their minds with painful visions. Screams of children. The cold emptiness of failed experiments. The endless suffering buried behind scientific masks.

Aarav shouted, "We came to end this!"

But it didn't want an end.

It wanted **silence.**

The Whisper of Freedom

Meher stood up, holding her spiritual beads tightly. She began chanting—slowly, steadily.

The entity screeched again, its form flickering. Vivaan activated his scanner, setting it to overload. The energy readings surged, surrounding the ghost with a bio-electromagnetic field.

"NOW!" Kiara screamed.

Meher's voice grew louder.

There was a final **blast of black mist**—and then…

Silence.

The Aftermath

When the team opened their eyes, the entity was gone.

So was the stain.

So was the cold.

The scanner was dead.

Kiara looked around and whispered, "Is it over?"

Rathod simply said, "We didn't destroy it… but we might have sent it back where it came from."

The Whisper Never Dies

Weeks later, Aarav found a handwritten letter outside his door.

"You silenced the whisper. But echoes always return."

Attached was a burnt page from the Project Void files—with one line underlined:

"Phase II: To be reactivated only upon psychic resonance."

The ghost… was not gone.

It was waiting.

End of Chapter 16

17

Resurrection Protocol

The Letter's Message

Aarav sat at his study table, holding the burnt paper tightly. The words "**Phase II: To be reactivated only upon psychic resonance**" kept echoing in his mind.

"Phase II?" Aarav muttered. "There's more?"

He immediately contacted Kiara, Vivaan, Kabir, Meher, and Dr. Rathod.

"We ended the ghost," Kiara said. "Didn't we?"

But Vivaan was pale. "No... we disrupted it. We never *destroyed* it."

Meher, still shaken by her past visions, whispered, "It never left. It was just sleeping."

Discovery of the Second Facility

Rathod revealed something no one knew.

"There was a backup lab—hidden even from most staff. It was only meant to activate if the first project failed. It was codenamed '**Subterra-Void**.'"

Aarav blinked. "And where is it?"

Rathod took out an old, folded blueprint. "Beneath the Proton Foundation's oldest research wing. Buried under layers of sealed concrete."

"And if the ghost is reawakening…" Vivaan added, "…that place might already be alive again."

Return to the Orphanage Grounds

To reach the hidden Subterra-Void lab, the team needed to go back to where it all started—**the orphanage**.

But this time, it wasn't just fear that gripped them—it was purpose.

As they entered the orphanage, the building moaned like a wounded beast. Myra's room, now quiet, held a strange glow.

Vivaan's scanner blinked faintly. "The readings are climbing again."

Suddenly, Kabir pointed to the wall.

"Myra's drawing… it's changed!"

The wall now had a drawing of a **dark tunnel**, a large black door, and an unknown figure **watching from the shadows.**

The Sealed Path

Inside the main hall, they noticed something new: a trapdoor beneath the old piano—**bolted shut with steel rods and chains**.

As they broke it open, Meher suddenly stopped.

"There's something… breathing down there."

Everyone froze.

But they had no choice.

One by one, they descended a rusty spiral staircase that went deeper than they had ever been. The deeper they went, the colder it got. It felt like the air itself didn't want them there.

Subterra-Void

They entered a massive underground space.

Walls of metal, flickering emergency lights, and broken containment pods surrounded them. On one wall, faded writing said:

"SUBTERRA-VOID: PHASE II — CONTROL THE MIND. KILL THE MEMORY."

Vivaan found a still-running console. Password protected.

"Let me try," Rathod said, typing nervously.

The system booted. Old logs flashed.

"...Subject-X's energy has fused with residual consciousness. It now manipulates not just spirits—but memory, thought, even time."

"...We lost control in Phase I. This time, we won't make the same mistake."

Possessed Reality

Suddenly, the corridor shifted. The walls began bleeding black liquid. The lights dimmed. Kabir screamed, "I saw my mother just now... she was here... she was crying!"

"It's a mental trap," Rathod shouted. "It's playing with our memories."

Meher collapsed again. Her eyes turned blank. "He... he's here. The one who doesn't belong..."

Vivaan checked her vitals—normal, but her brainwaves were spiking unnaturally.

"She's being controlled... but by what? The ghost?"

"No," Rathod said. "Something more."

Project: Resurrection Protocol

Vivaan found a locked vault labeled: **RESURRECTION PROTOCOL – DO NOT ACTIVATE**

Kabir: "If they labeled it like that, why build it at all?"

Rathod sighed. "Because science always wants a backup."

Inside, they found a floating, preserved **dark crystalline core**—still pulsing.

Beside it, a journal entry:

"Subject-X achieved fusion. It is no longer spirit or science. It's both. It protects the lie... and attacks the truth."

The truth began to sink in.

The Unknown Ghost was created to block outside discovery.

But now, it was feeding off all forms of awareness.

Confronting the Core

As they tried to shut down the console, the ghost returned—*larger, faster, more terrifying than ever.*

It slammed into the group. Kiara hit the ground, bleeding. Kabir was flung across the chamber.

Meher stood still, her body glowing.

"He's using me," she cried. "He's inside me!"

Vivaan made a snap decision.

"Reverse the signal. We can redirect his energy into the core!"

With Meher's consent, they activated the counter-signal through Vivaan's scanner.

The core glowed violently. A black wind swirled in the chamber.

The ghost screamed, but its body was **pulled into the core**, now glowing white.

Then... silence.

Is It Over?

Meher fell into Aarav's arms—exhausted but alive.

The core dimmed.

"Did it work?" Kiara asked.

"No sign of the ghost," Vivaan confirmed. "The scanner is clean."

They backed out, sealed the chamber, and returned to the surface.

But as they walked away, deep in the console, one last log was displayed:

"Resurrection Protocol complete. Entity stored. Awaiting new host."

Echoes Remain

Days later, a new construction crew came to demolish the old Proton building. One worker, while clearing the lower floor, found a **cracked glass vial** and a torn folder.

Before he could report it… the lights flickered.

A whisper echoed behind him.

"Truth… is death."

End of Chapter 17

18

Myra's Truth

Return to Silence

The days following their return from the Subterra-Void chamber were eerily quiet.

Aarav, Kiara, Meher, Kabir, and Vivaan had all gone back to their college, but none of them could focus. Their minds kept circling back to the orphanage, to the ghost, and to that **final log message**:

"Entity stored. Awaiting new host."

Vivaan sat alone in his room, replaying scanner footage. No signs of spirit activity.

But deep inside, they all felt it—**something was unfinished**.

And Meher... began dreaming again.

Myra's Dreams Begin

Meher jolted awake, soaked in sweat. Her voice cracked with panic.

"I saw her. Myra."

Aarav sat up beside her. "Another vision?"

"No," she whispered. "This time... she was crying. Not angry.

Crying like a scared child."

"She said, *'They never let me sleep. Not even after death.'*"

Meher's voice trembled.

"She wants us to know the full truth… *her truth.*"

Searching the Abandoned Records Room

The group gathered again and decided to visit the one place they hadn't fully explored—**the Proton Foundation's off-site Records Archive**, now abandoned and covered in vines.

They broke in.

Old files, folders, dusty shelves. Broken machines, damp walls, fungus, and rats.

Vivaan led with his scanner.

In the deepest corner, under a rotted wooden floor, they found a rusted metal box marked:

"CONFIDENTIAL – MYRA VERMA / EXPERIMENT B-12"

They opened it with shaking hands.

Inside: photographs, medical reports, a small diary… and a video tape labeled:

"Test Subject #27 — Psychic Response Monitoring"

Watching the Tape

They rushed to the college's old media lab. Vivaan set up the tape player.

The screen flickered.

A young girl—**Myra**—sat in a small sterile room, hooked to wires. Her face was pale. Scared.

A voice in the video—female, calm, professional.

"Day 14. Subject showing strong psychic activity under stress. Dreams recorded. Patterns forming."

Another video followed—Myra screaming in pain as sirens blared in the background.

"Do you see her?" the voice asked on tape.

Myra nodded, sobbing.

"The lady in the black smoke… she comes when I cry."

The screen glitched. Myra's eyes rolled back. And then…

"STOP THE PROCEDURE! SHE'S NOT RESPONDING—"

Static.

The room fell silent.

Kiara covered her mouth in horror. "She was never just a girl. She was their experiment."

Myra's Diary

Inside the box, they also found Myra's diary.

In child-like handwriting, Meher read aloud:

"They told me I was special. They said the voices I hear make me powerful. But I'm scared. I don't want to be powerful. I want to go home."

"I dream of a forest. It's always dark. And there's someone else there. He has no face. He hurts everyone. He tells me to be quiet."

"I miss Didi. I miss school. I miss laughing."

Meher broke down in tears.

"She didn't deserve this…"

Who Was the Faceless One?

Kabir finally said what everyone feared.

"The faceless one… It wasn't just a dream."

Kiara nodded slowly. "The unknown ghost… it used her, fed on her pain."

Vivaan looked stunned. "You're saying… he wasn't created by science. He *existed* before. And when they experimented on

Myra, she became the door for him?"

Dr. Rathod, now in hiding but still guiding them by messages, confirmed it:

"We never created that entity. We *found* it through her."

The Final Note in the Box

A final piece of folded paper fell out of the file. On it, Myra had written in red crayon:

"If you're reading this… please help me. He still walks. And I'm still here."

They looked at each other.

"She's still trapped?" Aarav asked.

Meher nodded slowly.

"She never left. She never got peace."

And then the lights in the lab flickered.

A faint whisper echoed through the room.

"Come back…"

One Last Mission

Aarav stood.

"We have to go back. To where it began."

"To Room 115," Kiara whispered.

"But this time," Vivaan added, "we don't fight the ghost. We help the girl."

"Rescue Myra," Meher said. "Set her free."

Everyone nodded.

The end was near.

But to reach it, they had to face **every horror they'd avoided so far.**

They packed, prepared, and took one final breath.

The last battle awaited.

End of Chapter 18

19

Room 115 – The Final Calling

The Return to Orphanage
The sun dipped behind the dark trees as the group returned to the orphanage one last time.

No one spoke. Their faces were pale, eyes heavy with the knowledge of what waited inside. Each step echoed with fear.

The gate creaked open on its own.

Vivaan shivered. "It knows we're here."

Room 115 had been silent for days, but now… a low, steady hum vibrated through the hallway, like a breathing machine deep underground.

The Sealed Door is Open
When they reached the hallway of Room 115, the door—previously sealed with chains and rusted locks—stood wide open.

A foul, cold wind blew from inside.

Carved into the wall in blood-like markings were the words:
"She waits. He watches."

Meher whispered, "This isn't just a haunted room. It's a

prison."

Entering the Room

The inside was not as they remembered.

It had changed.

The walls were covered in old drawings—childlike scribbles of forests, dark tunnels, faceless people. A small broken bed sat in the middle, and on the floor lay **Myra's old school shoes**, covered in dust.

Kabir stepped forward. "This… this was her room."

Suddenly, the lights blinked off. Only Kiara's flashlight remained.

And then—

A **low laugh** echoed.

Not Myra's.

A deeper, older laugh.

The Unknown Ghost Returns

Smoke filled the corners of the room. Dark, thick, pulsing.

Out of the smoke, a **figure formed. Faceless. Tall. Arms too long. Head tilted sideways.**

Meher screamed. The walls bled black fluid. The temperature dropped.

Vivaan's device crackled violently.

"ENTITY DETECTED. NOT HUMAN. NOT SPIRIT. NOT LOGICAL."

The unknown ghost moved slowly toward them, arms out.

But it didn't attack.

Instead, it turned… and pointed to a loose brick in the wall.

Aarav pulled it out.

Behind it—a tunnel.

The Forgotten Tunnel

The group entered the hidden tunnel. Dirt, decay, the stench of old chemicals.

Rats scurried past. The air was tight.

The tunnel was **a forgotten passageway** from the experiment room to Room 115. And at the very end—a small cell.

Inside, a **skeleton of a child** in a lab uniform. Next to it—a red diary.

Kiara opened it with shaking hands.

"They said I was broken. That I had too many voices. They tried to bury me here. But I'm still listening."

"The man without a face lives inside the machines. He promised me safety. But now I can't leave. I'm sorry."

It was Myra's final words.

The Truth Revealed

Vivaan finally understood.

"Myra wasn't haunting the orphanage. She was *trapped* between science and spirits. The ghost used her psychic mind as an anchor."

Kabir added, "The Proton Foundation's experiments made a door. But the real evil—the faceless one—was already waiting."

"He used her pain," Meher whispered. "And locked her soul here."

Breaking the Curse

Kiara stepped into the cell and held Myra's diary close.

"Listen to me, Myra," she said aloud. "You are not alone anymore. You are not broken. You were a child. You deserved peace."

A sudden **gust of wind** tore through the tunnel.

The faceless ghost screamed—its voice no longer powerful, but… scared.

The walls shook.

Meher, now connected to Myra through visions, said softly: "She's ready to leave… but he's stopping her."

Aarav lit the diary on fire.

Vivaan activated his device with a reverse-frequency pulse.

Suddenly, a **white light** burst from the fire.

A figure appeared—**Myra. Glowing. Crying.**

She smiled.

"I'm ready now…"

And then she was gone.

Collapse and Silence

The tunnel began to collapse. The group ran.

As they exited Room 115, the entire corridor behind them crumbled.

The orphanage fell into deep silence.

No more whispers. No more footsteps. Just peace.

Myra is Free

Outside, the air smelled clean. The weight had lifted.

Meher looked to the sky.

"She's gone."

Kiara smiled faintly. "And that… thing?"

Aarav nodded. "We didn't destroy it. But we closed the door."

The Final Message

Back in college, they received one last anonymous email.

Just a blank page.

Except for one sentence:

"The void never forgets."

Aarav closed the laptop. "It's over."

"But is it really?" Kabir whispered.

They all knew… in some corner of the world, **the darkness still watches.**

But for now…

Room 115 was silent.

End of Chapter 19

Epilogue

Ten Years Later

It had been ten years since the haunting at the Proton Orphanage.

The land where the building once stood was now overgrown with trees. Nature had taken over. There was no sign that a building ever existed there—no brick, no wood, no gate.

Only silence.

Kiara stood at the edge of the forest, staring at the place where **Room 115** once was. She wore a long coat now, older, wiser, but still carrying the same fire in her eyes.

She wasn't here as a student anymore.

She was here as a **writer**—finishing a story that never truly ended.

The Book: "Secrets of Room 115"

Kiara's book had just been published—*"Secrets of Room 115"*. It was a fictionalized account, but the truth was hidden between the lines.

In the story, names were changed. The orphanage was only called "The House." The ghost was called "The Watcher."

But those who knew… would know.

Her book became a **bestseller**.

People loved the mystery. The fear. The emotional pain. The truth hidden in plain sight.

But no one truly believed it was real.

Except those who were there.

The Group Reunites

One evening, Kiara met with Aarav, Meher, Vivaan, and Kabir at a quiet café in Delhi.

They smiled, shared memories, laughed about their old days… but they all knew what haunted them.

Vivaan now worked in bio-research, helping orphans with genetic conditions.

Meher taught meditation and spiritual therapy.

Kabir became a writer too, but for documentaries.

Aarav? He disappeared into forest conservation. He said trees were "less complicated."

But in their silence, they all knew they'd seen **something** no one else ever would.

A Final Visit

After the meeting, Kiara returned to the orphanage land one last time.

She lit a candle.

Set it on the ground.

Then whispered, "Thank you, Myra. You saved us."

A wind blew gently.

The flame flickered.

And in that moment… she heard it.

A faint **giggle**.

Like a child playing in the distance.

She smiled softly. "Rest now."

And turned to walk away.

But in the Darkness...

Far underground, deeper than any map ever showed...

A cold, flickering light glowed inside a **sealed metal chamber**.

Old wires sparked. Dust floated in the air.

And on the wall—a name slowly appeared, written in frost:

"Raghav."

Then, a whisper:

"One was saved... but I still remember."

A dark shadow passed the camera.

And silence returned.

THE END